PLAY BY PLAY
GOLF

Golf instructor Peter Krause and the following athletes were photographed for this book:
- Nick Berg,
- Gabe Hilmoe,
- Matt Hilmoe,
- Sarah Hilmoe,
- Angie Rizzo,
- Reed Tauer,
- Jenny Tollette.

LERNER
SPORTS
AN IMPRINT OF LERNER PUBLISHING GROUP

PLAY BY PLAY
GOLF

Peter Krause

Photographs by Andy King

Lerner Publications Company • Minneapolis

To my parents, Mel and Kay, for their love and support and to Darrell Guay, who introduced a young boy to the wonderful game of golf.

Copyright © 2002 by Lerner Publications Company

All rights reserved. International copyright secured. No part of this book may be reproduced, stored in a retrieval system, or transmitted in any form or by any means—electronic, mechanical, photocopying, recording, or otherwise—without the prior written permission of Lerner Publications Company, except for the inclusion of brief quotations in an acknowledged review.

LernerSports
An imprint of Lerner Publishing Group
241 First Avenue North
Minneapolis, MN 55401 U.S.A.

Website address: www.lernerbooks.com

Library of Congress Cataloging-in-Publication Data

Krause, Peter, 1954–
   Play-by-play golf / by Peter Krause ; photographs by Andy King.
      p. cm. — (Play-by-play)
   Includes bibliographical references (p.) and index.
   Summary: Details tips and practice drills for golf, as well as information on the sport's history and equipment.
   ISBN 0–8225–0076–0 (pbk. : alk. paper)
   1. Golf—Juvenile literature. [1. Golf.] I. King, Andy, ill. II. Title. III. Series.
GV968.K73 2002
796.352—dc21
                                                        2001005911

Manufactured in the United States of America
1 2 3 4 5 6 – JR – 07 06 05 04 03 02

Photo Acknowledgments
Photographs are reproduced with the permission of: pp. 7, 9 (top), The Saint Andrew's Golf Club; p. 8, Trustees of the British Museum; p. 9 (bottom), USGA; p. 10, Rick Dole/Golden Bear International; p. 11, Dee Darden; p. 14, Nancy Smedstad/IPS, Courtesy of Tim Nelson; p. 19, Edvins Erkmanis. All diagrams by Laura Westlund.

CONTENTS

Chapter 1 ....How This Game Got Started 7
Chapter 2 ....Basics 13
Chapter 3 ....The Swing 19
Chapter 4 ....The Way to Play 31
Chapter 5 ....Skill Shots 39
Chapter 6 ....On the Course.....................................51
Golf Talk 61
Further Reading 63
Index 64

Chapter 1

HOW THIS GAME GOT STARTED

When you think of playing a game, what comes to your mind? Fun, excitement, challenge, competition? Most of the games we play require up to 10 other participants. There is a game, however, that meets all these expectations and that you can play alone or with other people. That game is golf.

Hitting a golf ball doesn't take a lot of strength or athletic ability. Because of this, golfers come in every size, shape, age, and skill level. The challenge of golf is that you have to think about and plan your shots. And even then, there's always something new to surprise you.

Taken in 1888, this is one of the first photographs of golf being played in the United States.

Paul Sandby painted this watercolor picture of golfers in 1746.

As early as A.D. 1100, Roman shepherds hit stones or feather-filled leather balls in their fields with curved sticks. This early version of golf—called paganica—eventually made its way to Scotland, where it became the game we know as golf. There are also records of golf-like games being played in Holland in the thirteenth century and in Chile in the sixteenth century.

In 1744 the Honourable Company of Edinburgh Golfers in Edinburgh, Scotland, made up the first formal rules of the game. Back then, golf was played alongside the ocean on sandy areas of land called "**links**." The term links is still used to describe a golf **course.**

The game's popularity grew with the British Empire. Wherever the British went to establish a new colony, they took their game of golf with them. Golf began in America in the original thirteen colonies.

In 1888 John Reid, an American from Scotland, asked his friend in Scotland, Tom Morris Sr., to send him a set of golf clubs. Back then, no factories produced golf clubs; they had to be made by hand. Morris was well known for the golf clubs he made. Reid was so happy with the clubs Morris sent that he persuaded some of his friends to try them. Morris was soon sending clubs to the United States as fast as he could make them.

This interest in the game led Reid and his friends to build the United States's first golf course, in Yonkers, New York. It consisted of three **holes** in a pasture, which they later expanded to six holes in an orchard.

John Reid (left) helped introduce Americans to the game of golf in the late 1800s.

Theodore Havemeyer (in the straw hat) was the first president of the United States Golf Association (USGA).

JACK NICKLAUS

Jack Nicklaus began playing golf when he was 10 years old by tagging along with his dad. When Jack was 13, he won the Ohio State Junior Championship. Eight years later, Jack joined the Professional Golfers' Association (PGA) tour.

Jack, whose nickname is the "Golden Bear," has won more than 70 tournaments. He has won the Masters Tournament, one of the most prestigious American tournaments, six times. He now plays on the Senior tour and designs golf courses.

In 1893 Charles MacDonald built the first 18-hole golf course in the United States. The United States Golf Association (USGA) was created in 1894 to organize and govern the fast-growing sport. The USGA still sets the official rules for golf competition.

At the turn of the century, professional golfers from Scotland and England were coming to the United States to build golf clubs and courses. Rodman Wanamaker, a department store tycoon, held a luncheon in 1916 for the top professional and amateur golfers of New York. They decided to form a national organization to promote the game and the career of golf professional. This was the birth of the Professional Golfers' Association of America (PGA).

There are 25 million golfers and more than 23,000 golf professionals in the United States. These professionals introduce new players to the game and help them develop their playing skills. Golfers can use their skills on nearly 16,000 golf courses in the United States.

Some golfers play for cash prizes on professional tours. The male pros play on the PGA tour. Women professionals compete on the Ladies Professional Golf Association (LPGA) tour, which began in 1948.

Many people play golf to relax or to enjoy the fresh air. They like trying to

NANCY LOPEZ

Nancy Lopez's father took her golfing when she was eight years old. Nancy won her first tournament the following year, and she continues to win.

Nancy loved many sports as a child, but golf quickly became her favorite. When she was 16, Nancy was the top-ranked amateur golfer in the United States. Her high school didn't have a girls' golf team, but Nancy led the boys' team to two state championships. After high school, Nancy went to Tulsa University, where she won the national collegiate championship.

Nancy joined the Ladies Professional Golf Association (LPGA) tour in 1977 when she was 21 years old. Nancy still competes on the LPGA tour and is already in the LPGA Hall of Fame.

---

improve their skills and master new ones. For those who want to compete against other golfers, there are high school and college teams and recreational leagues.

Whether you are playing alone or with others, playing golf will challenge your physical and mental skills. Golf fascinates many people because it pits the golfer against the course. No one is trying to tackle you, block your shot, or make you miss a pitch. It is up to you to decide how you want to hit the ball. Then you must carry out that decision. Doing that can be a challenge.

Chapter 2

BASICS

To play a round of golf, you will need a set of clubs, golf balls, and shoes that are acceptable to wear on the golf course. Golf clubs are expensive. Before you spend your money, be sure you know what clubs you want to buy. Borrow clubs from a friend or relative. Nancy Lopez, a professional golfer who has won more than 40 tournaments, learned to play as a kid by using one of her mother's clubs to play the entire course. Or you can rent clubs at most courses. Ask the course pro for some clubs that fit your size and skill level. Once you are sure what kind of clubs you like—and you have saved enough money—ask the pro to help you choose clubs to buy.

GOLF SHOES

Golf shoes have short steel spikes that dig into the ground and keep your feet from slipping on the grass. You can also wear gym shoes that have a good tread.

GOLF BALLS

A golf ball weighs 1.62 ounces and is 1.68 inches in diameter. It is made in one of three forms: solid, two, or three piece.

A solid-piece ball is molded out of a durable, synthetic material. It is good for beginners and is used on practice ranges.

A two-piece ball is a rubber ball covered in Surlyn®, a plastic substance that is made by the DuPont Company. This ball is durable and gives the golfer good distance and control over the shot.

A three-piece ball is small and has rubber bands wrapped tightly around it. The outer cover is a rubber material called balata—the dried sap from a West Indian tree or its synthetic version. Professionals and very good golfers use balata balls.

They travel farther than the other types but are more likely to get damaged.

All golf balls have a dimpled outer cover to help control the flight of the ball by affecting the way air flows around it. The more dimples on a ball, the lower and straighter its flight will be. Markings and colors help golfers identify their balls.

Golf is a game of distance and direction. A set of clubs has at least 3 **woods,** 10 **irons,** and a **putter.** Each club is designed to provide a specialized degree of distance and direction. The variety helps a golfer accurately place a shot.

On the first shot, the ball should go far and straight. Woods are designed to accomplish this. Woods are the longest clubs and have the biggest hitting surface. When golf began, wood was the easiest material to make into a club. Most modern clubs—even woods—are made of steel.

As the ball gets closer to the hole, it needs to go high and not too far. An iron will launch the ball high into the air so when it lands, it won't roll very far from the hole.

Once near the hole, a putter hits it into the **cup.** The putter doesn't lift the ball off the ground but helps it roll along the putting surface.

Each club has a handle, a shaft, and a clubhead. When you look at woods and irons, you will notice a distinct difference in their design and shape. Woods have longer shafts than irons. The clubheads on woods are shaped like half-moons. An iron's clubhead looks like an open hand tilted back toward the ground. Irons have grooves running across the face of the clubhead. They make the ball spin backward. This backspin makes the ball stop when it lands on the grass.

When you hold an iron or wood with the clubhead touching the ground, the top of the clubhead will

Wood **Iron** **Putter**

be tilted away from the bottom of the clubhead. This tilt is called **loft.** The more loft in a club, the higher the ball will travel. To let golfers know how high and how far, numbers are stamped on the bottom of the clubs. Woods are numbered from 1 to 5. Irons are numbered from 1 to 10. Putters have the least amount of loft and are not numbered.

High-numbered clubs hit the ball high but not very far. Low-numbered clubs hit the ball far but not high. For example, a 9-iron, which has a lot of loft, will hit the ball higher into the air than a 4-iron. But the 4-iron, a longer club with less loft, will make the ball go farther than a 9-iron. Generally, there is a 10-yard difference between the average shot a good golfer hits with each iron and 15 yards between shots with each wood.

Each club's clubhead has a **toe,** a **face,** and a **heel.** The ball will fly the straightest when it is struck with the face of the club. When a golf ball is hit properly with the center of the club face, it will spin backward as it is traveling toward the target. This helps the ball go straight toward the target.

If the ball is struck with the toe of the club behind the heel, the ball will spin from left to right. The ball's flight will

PITCHING AND SAND WEDGES

A pitching wedge is used 100 yards or less from the hole to lob the ball over trees, sand, water, and mounds. The ball will land softly and not roll very far.

Sand wedges are used primarily to hit out of sand and tall grass. A sand wedge's wide, flat bottom, called the flange, slides through sand and under the ball.

curve to the right of a right-handed golfer and to the left for a left-handed golfer. This is called a **slice.** If the toe of the club is in front of the heel when it hits the ball, the ball will spin from right to left. The ball's flight will curve to the left of a right-handed golfer for a **hook.**

Chapter 3

THE SWING

What makes playing golf really enjoyable is being able to hit the ball consistently toward a target. It is frustrating to swing with all of your energy and effort and watch helplessly as the ball curves away from where you wanted it to go.

By learning how to swing correctly, and then swinging that way every time, you can increase your chances of putting the ball where you want it to go. But even then, the wind, the ground the ball is on, and the club you're using will conspire to surprise you. That is golf's challenge.

Just as no two people are alike, neither are any two golf swings alike. A swing is determined by the golfer's height, arm length, and athletic ability. There are three elements, however, that should go into every swing: the **grip,** the **set-up,** and a mental image of the correct swing.

A TIGER WITH HIS WOODS

Tiger Woods dominates the golf world. At the 1997 Masters Tournament, his first major tournament as a professional, he impressed his fans and fellow pros by winning with the lowest score in history, 270. Tiger turned pro in 1996, won six PGA events within 12 months, and hasn't stopped winning since.

HOME ON THE RANGE

Most public courses have practice ranges. Practice ranges separate from courses often have putting greens, too.

At the range, you rent a bucket of balls and find an open space. Everyone hits in the same direction, often at targets posted at various distances from the hitting line.

The practice range is the perfect place to fine-tune your swing or try out a different style or a new club. It's also a fun way to keep your golf muscles in shape if you can't play a round.

THE GRIP

For Nick to strike the ball with the face of the club, he must put his hands on the handle correctly. Nick is right-handed, so he places the fingers of his right hand on the club where the handle and shaft meet. Then, he lifts the club up to his waist with the toe of the club pointing to the sky.

Nick brings up his left hand and "shakes hands" with the end of the handle. If you look closely, his left thumb and forefinger look like they are squeezing the trigger of a squirt gun. He slides his right hand up the handle toward the left hand. His right pinky overlaps his left forefinger, the rest of his hand covers up the left thumb. His right thumb and forefinger also look as if they are squeezing a trigger.

If Nick were left-handed, he would do the same thing but with the opposite hands. Using this grip, Nick can hit the ball with the face of the golf club. Variations of this grip, even small ones, will lead to shots that are struck off the toe or heel of the clubhead and land in the rough.

THE SET-UP

To aim the club correctly, first find your target. Next, think of a railroad track. Imagine that the ball is on the outside rail, on a line going to your target. Imagine that you are standing on the inside rail, with your feet, knees, hips, and shoulders all an equal distance from the outside rail.

Nick is in this position. With his club in front of his waist, Nick bends from his hips, just as if he were about to bow to someone. His knees are bent, and his weight is on the balls of his feet.

In the photograph, you can see that Nick's coach has stuck a yellow pole in the ground at the correct angle for Nick's club. Using the stick as a guide, Nick can make sure his club and body are in the correct position for his swing.

THE MENTAL IMAGE

Now that Nick is ready to swing, he pictures in his mind a good swing. Nick visualizes a golf swing that is a combination of two motions—circular and up-and-down.

Because Nick is standing alongside the ball, his club will be swung around his body in a semi-circular motion. Since the ball is on the

Downswing

Backswing

Follow-through

Takeaway

Impact

START

END

ground, Nick will have to swing the club in an up-and-down motion.

The trick to swinging the club correctly is mixing the right amount of each motion. When Nick correctly blends the two motions, he hits the ball with the club face positioned toward the target. The golf club itself helps Nick. Notice the angle at which the shaft comes out of the clubhead and up into Nick's hands. Nick's swing should resemble this angle.

THE SWING

There are five basic parts to a golf swing. Nick will illustrate where the club needs to be in each position.

The most critical part of Nick's swing is the **takeaway,** which is when Nick moves his club away from the ball. Nick moves his hands, arms, and shoulders as a unit. At the beginning of the takeaway, the club stays in front of Nick's body as it moves up. As his arms and shoulders turn around his spine, the shaft of the club is parallel to the target when the club is parallel to the ground.

Nick can practice by watching his swing in a mirror. The more Nick can see himself swing the club into this position, the easier it will become for him to repeat this on the course.

On the **backswing,** Nick cocks his wrists and, at the same time, slightly turns his left forearm. This puts the club parallel to its original starting position. All the while, his shoulders are turning around his spine until his back faces the target. Nick also shifts most of his weight to his right leg. This coiling motion will supply the power needed to hit the ball toward the target.

At the top of his swing, the club is parallel with the ground and the target. Nick is now ready to swing the club back down to the ball on a line that resembles the backswing.

The **downswing** brings the club to the ball on the same path it went up. To do this, Nick moves his hips, legs, and knees as if he were skipping a stone across a pond. This lateral movement shifts his body weight from his right leg to his left leg.

As his lower body begins its movement, Nick's hands and arms drop down in toward his right side. This puts the club at an angle parallel to the angle it was in at the set-up position. To keep the club moving toward the ball at this angle, Nick begins to uncock his wrists. This allows the club to pass through the same position in the takeaway—parallel with the target and the ground. Now the club face is in position to hit the ball.

At the **point of impact,** Nick finds out if he has swung the club correctly. The club face should face the target

THE SWING'S THE THING

To practice the proper golf swing, place two golf balls 18 inches apart. Swing the clubhead up and over the back ball. On the downswing, concentrate on swinging the clubhead on a path just inside of the back ball. If the shots go to the right of your target, turn your forearms a little sooner so you strike the ball with the clubhead facing the target.

as it strikes the ball. For this to happen, the back of Nick's left hand must also face the target.

As the golf club approaches the ball, Nick rotates his left forearm back to its original starting position. This rotation allows the back of his left hand to face the target at impact. Also, notice how Nick's hips have turned out of the way. This allows his legs, knees, and his right foot to move toward the target, like the motion of a pitcher throwing to home plate.

For a balanced finish, Nick's **follow-through** must swing the club through the correct position. Just as in the takeaway, after hitting the ball Nick swings the club so that it is parallel with the target when it is parallel with the ground. Because he has so much momentum in his swing, his arms will continue to swing up and around.

After he completes his swing, Nick's shoulders, hips, and knees face the target. His arms have swung across his chest, and his club is over his left shoulder. He finishes the swing with most of his weight on his left foot and his right foot up on its toe.

Even though it took several minutes to read how to swing a golf club, it only takes a couple of seconds to do it. Practice the various positions of the swing one at a time and at your own pace. But when it comes to swinging the club while playing, trust what you've worked on and believe in yourself.

Once you have learned how to swing correctly, you can hit the ball with any club—except the putter—using this swing. The club you use will determine how far the ball will travel.

Like other athletic moves, the golf swing can be graceful and artistic. To achieve such grace, start the club back slowly from the ball and gradually increase the speed of your swing. Swing the club as fast as possible through impact.

With time and practice, you will master the golf swing. Patience and practice are the main things you need to learn the correct fundamentals.

IRON OUT A ROUTINE

To start your practice sessions, hit with the wedge, then the 9-, 8-, and 7-irons. These short irons are used to hit accurate shots. Once you are warmed up, hit with the longer clubs. Go slow, trying to hit the ball hard too soon can lead to an incorrect swing.

Chapter 4

THE WAY TO PLAY

Baseball games last for nine innings. Football games are divided into four quarters. In each sport the team with the most points wins. Golf is different.

THE COURSE

Golfers try to use the fewest possible **strokes** to hit a ball into a small opening in the ground. Both the opening and the area of the course you play on before reaching it are called a hole. A golf course has 9 or 18 of these holes, separated by yards of grass. The golfers play each hole in order. There is no set time limit for a golfer to play a hole. Called a **round,** 18 holes make up a complete game. The term round came from the early golf courses built in Scotland. Many were laid out in a circle with the starting and finishing points near each other.

GETTING BETTER

To become a better golfer, you have several options. The professionals at most courses give private lessons for a fee.

Many community education programs and recreation centers offer golf classes or group lessons. Check with your physical education teacher.

Golf camps often advertise in golfing magazines. Search the pages for a camp that sounds right for you. Or, stay home and borrow instructional videos from the library or video store. And don't forget to practice!

Each hole is made up of a **tee box,** a **fairway,** the **rough, hazards,** and a **green.** The tee box is where you begin to play each hole. The ball must be hit between the two markers that define the tee box. Often there are three sets of markers—red markers for women, white for men, and blue markers for professionals or tournament players.

You may hit the first ball of a hole off a **tee.** All other shots on the hole are played off of the ground. The shot hit when teeing off is also called a **drive.**

The fairway extends between the tee box and the green. Its grass is cut to a height of only 1 to 2 inches. The rough surrounds the fairway, and its

TOURNAMENT TIME

There are two ways a round of golf can be contested—stroke play or match play. In a stroke-play tournament, the winner is determined by the lowest number of strokes or by subtracting the players' handicaps from their scores.

Match play is played by holes. The object of match play is to win more holes than your opponent. The players' scores on each hole are used to determine who wins the hole.

For example, if Jeff makes a 3 on the first hole and Bob scores a 5, Jeff wins the hole and is one hole up. If, on the second hole, Bob makes a 2 and Jeff makes a 7, Bob wins the hole and the match is even. The match is played over 18 holes.

than the fairway grass. Found on the green, the cup is 4¼ inches in diameter and 4 inches deep. A removable 6-foot pole called a **pin,** or flagstick, shows golfers the cup's location.

SCORING

Holes generally vary in length from 100 to 600 yards. Holes that are less than 250 yards long are expected to be played by a skilled golfer in three shots. Holes that are 250 to 475 yards are meant to be played in four strokes. Holes longer than 475 yards are supposed to be played in five shots.

grass is 3 to 6 inches high. Bushes and trees may be in the rough. **Out of bounds** may look like the rough but a sign or white poles usually mark the area. Hazards are ponds, streams, and sand traps. Hazards add challenge. Water hazards are marked with red or yellow poles.

The grass on the green is cut shorter

GOLF'S HANDICAP SYSTEM

To allow people of various skill levels to compete against one another, a **handicap** system is used. For instance, let's say Joe averages a score of 95 for 18 holes—23 shots higher than par. So his handicap is 23. If Joe shoots a 93 for 18 holes during handicap play, he subtracts 23 from his score for a net score of 70. He beat the par-72 course by two shots.

Handicaps range from 0 to 36. A golfer's handicap is based on his or her skill level and the difficulty of the course. Golfers turn in their scorecards to the professional after playing a round. These scores are recorded, and their handicaps are figured.

The expected number of strokes is called **par.** You measure your score against par. If you use that many strokes to play a hole, you shot par, or parred the hole. If you play a hole with one stroke less than par, you have shot a **birdie.** Two shots better than par is called an **eagle.** When you take one stroke more than par, you have shot a **bogey.** Two shots over par is a double bogey, three shots over is a triple bogey, and so on.

The par number always includes two putts. For example, a par-3 hole means that a top-notch golfer is expected to hit a tee shot to the green and **putt** twice to finish the hole. On a par-5 hole, that golfer is supposed to take three shots to get the ball on the green before putting twice.

A typical golf course has 4 par-3 holes, 4 par-5 holes and 10 par-4 holes. The 18 pars add up to 72. So, the goal is to shoot a score lower than 72.

Of course, when you are learning to play you will have different goals. You may want to keep your score on each hole to 10 or better. Maybe you will try to keep your total score under 120. Shooting par challenges all but the very best golfers. Don't get discouraged if par seems a long way off. Do your best, one shot at a time, and you will keep improving.

RULES AND ETIQUETTE

When a player breaks a rule in golf, a shot is added to his or her score as a penalty. For example, Angie has hit her ball into the water and can't play the shot. She must take a penalty of one shot. She can either retrieve her ball from the water or, if the ball is too far in the pond to recover, use a new ball. Angie drops the ball within one club length of where her shot went into the water.

Sarah has a different problem. Her ball is up against a tree and she can't hit it. She takes a penalty of one shot to move her ball away from the tree (but not closer to the cup). Unlike other sports, the golfer, not an umpire, decides that a rule has been broken. That's why golf is a great game for developing your character!

Golf also has its own special set of manners, or etiquette. Be quiet and still while others are making their shots. Don't walk between the cup and another player's ball on the green. Congratulate a player on a good shot, but don't offer advice after a bad one. If there's any chance your ball could hit a person playing in front of you, don't swing. If, after you've hit your ball, you see someone who could get hit by it, yell "Fore!" to warn them.

The rules of golf allow up to four people to play a hole at one time. The person with the lowest score on the previous hole is the first one to tee off on the next hole. (You can flip a coin to see who hits first on the No. 1 tee box.) While playing a hole, the person whose ball is farthest from the cup hits first. This order of play is followed until the hole is completed by all players.

There is no time limit in golf, but golf etiquette calls for golfers to keep their game moving along. It usually takes four hours to play 18 holes of golf. Don't rush your shots, but don't dawdle between shots. Always be ready when it is your turn to play. Watch your ball and those of your partners. If a ball goes into the rough, try to notice something, like an oddly shaped tree or a bend in the fairway, near where you last saw the ball. Using that marker, you can find the ball without a long search.

When playing a round of golf, keep pace with the group in front of yours. If you are falling behind or if you've lost a ball, allow the group behind you to "play through" your group. Let that group tee off on the next hole before your group. Or, when on the green of a par-3 hole, wave so that the golfers behind you know that they can hit their shots onto the green. Then, allow them to finish the hole before you complete your play.

Learning to play quickly can be beneficial, especially in a tournament. In a tournament, an official times every golfer's play. If the official decides you are playing too slowly, he or she will add two shots to your final score. Even when you're not in a tournament, playing slowly might annoy the players in your group and those playing behind you.

MARKING YOUR PUTT

On the green, if your ball is between another golfer's ball and the cup, you must move it according to the rules. You are also allowed to pick up your ball and clean it off before putting. Before you pick up your ball, slide a coin behind it to mark your position. When you are ready to putt, replace the ball and pick up the coin.

Chapter 5

SKILL SHOTS

There is more to golf than full swings. Some of the skill shots, such as chipping and pitching, use the full golf swing as a starting point. But putting demands different skills. Learning these advanced shots takes time and effort. Mastering them will make you a good golfer.

CHIPS

When a golfer is within 10 feet of the green, he or she will hit a short, low shot called a **chip.** The object is to hit the ball out of the long grass and just onto the green. Once on the green, the ball will roll like a putt. You want the ball to finish as near to the cup as possible. With a good chip, you'll only need one putt to sink the ball in the cup. You can use a 7-, 8-, or 9-iron to chip.

To execute the shot, Matt grips farther down the handle than he would for a full swing and leans his body and club toward the cup. He strikes the ball with the motion of a pendulum. There is very little follow-through on a chip, so Matt's club stops soon after he hits the ball. The ball pops up into the air and lands on the green.

PITCH SHOTS

Often you will find yourself in situations where there is a sand trap, or **bunker,** between you and the hole. A chip shot would not work in this case because the ball would not roll through the sand. You need to hit a shot that flies over the bunker, lands on the green, and doesn't roll very far. This is called a **pitch** shot.

A pitch shot makes the ball fly farther in the air than it would roll on the ground. The shot looks like the path of a pitched horseshoe. When the ball is lofted in the air, it will not have enough momentum to roll like a chip would.

Gabe uses a 10-iron to hit a pitch shot. His grip is toward the bottom of the handle. He aims the clubhead at his target. His body and club lean slightly toward the cup.

Gabe moves the club back from the ball with a slight cocking of his wrists. As he starts his downswing, his knees move toward the target. Meanwhile, his wrists uncock toward the ball. When he hits the ball, the loft of the club makes the ball go up.

Gabe swings the club well past the point of impact for a full follow-through. The ball flies high into the air and lands softly on the green.

PUTTS

Putting occurs on the closely mown area of the golf course called the green. Putting is very challenging because the green is not flat. A green has miniature slopes and hills that will cause the ball to roll on curved paths.

When putting, you must judge how hard to hit the ball and what path the ball should take to the cup. The slower the ball rolls, the more it curves because of the slope. For example, Matt is 20 feet from the hole. The green he is on has a 2-foot slope from right to left. Matt has to start the ball rolling 2 feet to the right of the cup with the proper speed to make it go in.

READING THE GREEN

To determine how much a putt will curve, notice how the green slopes and decide how hard to hit the ball. The ball will always curve away from the highest point. The speed of the putt will determine how straight it rolls. The faster the ball, the straighter it goes.

There are many different putting styles, just as there are many different full swings. But a putting stroke should be very simple, much simpler than a full swing.

Jenny is holding the handle. Notice how both of her thumbs are pointing down at the clubhead. She aims the clubhead on the path she wants the ball to start rolling. As she swings the putter, Jenny imagines her hands, arms, and shoulders are a pendulum. This pendular motion makes the putter move straight back from the ball and straight to it. With practice, Jenny has learned how hard to hit her putts.

PRACTICE PUTTS

Here's a drill that will help you learn how hard you should hit your putts. Line up five golf balls in a row. Take five steps from the balls and by each step, place a tee in the ground. Go back to the row of balls and try to hit the first ball to the first tee. Then hit the second ball to the second tee, and repeat this with the rest of the golf balls. Practice this drill from 10, 15, and 20 steps to learn how to hit just hard enough to make the putt.

BUNKER SHOTS

Bunkers, or sand traps, are often found alongside a green. In a bunker, start your shot with the clubhead at least one inch above the sand. A **penalty stroke** is assessed if your club touches the sand before you swing to hit the ball. The object of the shot is to hit the sand two inches behind the ball and allow the club to slide underneath the ball. The buildup of sand between the ball and clubhead propels the ball out of the bunker and onto the green.

If possible, use a sand wedge to hit

a shot out of the bunker. The bottom of a sand wedge is lower than other iron bottoms. This allows the clubhead to slide through the sand. If you don't have a sand wedge, use a 9-iron or pitching wedge.

Reed starts his bunker shot with the proper grip. He digs his feet into the sand to keep his balance. His feet point toward the left of the cup. Reed aims the clubhead at the cup.

Reed swings as he would for any other full swing. He swings very hard because he will hit sand instead of the ball. Reed follows through so that the sand doesn't slow the clubhead. The ball floats out of the bunker and lands softly on the green.

Chapter 6

ON THE COURSE

Learning the proper swing techniques and various shots will take plenty of practice. Practice will help you shoot a low score and will also prepare you for the challenges on the golf course. When playing, you must manage the wind, avoid the sand and water, and deal with the pressure of putting. Let's see how Nick, Reed, Sarah, and Jenny put this practice into action.

The foursome are about to play a par-4 hole that is 385 yards long. Golf courses have men's tee boxes and women's tee boxes. Because most women don't hit the ball as far as most men, the women's tee boxes are closer to the hole. Nick and Reed will tee off first because their tee box is farther from the hole.

WARMING UP

Before you play any sport, including golf, you need to warm up. A simple stretching exercise is to place a club behind your back between your elbows. Spread your feet shoulder width apart and turn right and left. Then place the club behind your back under your armpits. Repeat the same twisting motion. Finally, bend from your waist and touch the ground. In just a few minutes, your muscles are stretched and ready to swing.

HOLE IN ONE!

A **hole in one** is rare! A golfer needs skill to be able to hit the ball so accurately that it goes in with one shot, but most golfers agree that luck is the main ingredient. Holes in one occur primarily on par 3 holes, but they have also been made on par 4s. A hole in one on a par 3 is called an eagle. On a par 4, it is called a double eagle.

As Nick prepares for his tee shot, his eye catches the bunker to the left of the fairway and the trees to the right of it. He feels the wind blowing from right to left and so plans to hit the ball down the right side. He places his hands firmly on the handle and positions his body and clubhead toward the right of the fairway. The club gradually builds up speed to launch the ball down the fairway. The ball explodes off the club face and blasts down the right side of the fairway. The wind blows the ball to the left. It lands in the middle of the fairway. Jenny says, "Nice shot!"

Next Reed puts his ball on a tee. He steps back and swings his No. 1 wood, or driver, several times. As he steps up to the ball, he wiggles the club to get comfortable. Reed slowly brings back the driver, then whips it down to hit the ball. The ball flies off the tee, which shatters at the impact. Reed's spirits sink as he watches the ball's flight curve to the right, slicing into the rough.

Now it's Sarah's turn. She takes a couple of practice swings by the women's tee while she pictures the flight of her ball down the middle of the fairway. Sarah carefully positions the clubhead and her body to execute a smooth, fluid swing. Her efforts are rewarded with a long, straight drive.

Jenny is the last to tee off. After several practice swings, she gets into her set-up position. She takes a deep breath, blows it out, and begins her takeaway. Whipping the club to the ball, Jenny drives the ball forcefully off the tee. But when she looks up, Jenny sees her ball land in the rough.

"C'mon Jen," Reed calls as he slings his bag of clubs over his shoulder. "You can keep me company. At least you didn't slice it as bad as I did."

Nick and Sarah walk down the fairway for their second shots. As they approach their tee shots, they look to see where their balls are in relation to the 150-yard marker. Many golf courses have plates on the fairway indicating how far you are from the green.

DIVOT DUTY

When hitting a shot with an iron on the fairway, quite often your clubhead will tear out some turf. This **divot** must be put back in the ground.

If the divot came from ahead of your ball, you're hitting correctly. If the divot came out before you hit the ball, you goofed. Your swing loses a lot of power if the club hits the ground before it hits the ball. Often this happens if you try to scoop up the ball. Remember, the club's loft is designed to do this for you. Just relax, take a deep breath, and try to swing the club smoothly.

Jenny finds her ball among some small trees. It is about even with Sarah's, but because it curved to the right, it's farther from the hole. Reed, meanwhile, finds his ball even farther to the right than Jenny's, but 20 yards closer to the hole than Nick's ball. Jenny will hit first.

Jenny decides to use a 7-iron. She wants to hit the ball high and far so it can clear the sand bunker in front of the green. Jenny swings and hits the ball solidly, but her troubles continue. The wind blows her ball into the bunker. "Tough luck Jen," Sarah calls from the fairway. "But you're good in the sand!"

Sarah closes her eyes for a moment and pictures the 7-iron shot she wants to hit. Then she steps up to the ball, takes a deep breath, and swings. It's a beautiful shot, heading straight for the pin. The ball lands on the fairway, just a couple of yards in front of the green. "Nice shot Sarah! You're hot today!" Jenny says.

Nick chooses to use his 9-iron for his second shot. His strong, balanced swing produces a solid shot. He looks up to see his ball tracking down the flagstick like a guided missile. The ball lands softly on the green, and rolls until it is just 15 feet from the cup.

Reed's ball is nestled in some tall, thick grass in the rough. To power it out of the grass, he picks his 9-iron. Reed's swing is solid, but the ball is held up by the wind and lands in the bunker, just 5 feet from Jenny's. "You don't have to keep me company, Reed," Jenny teases. "Didn't want you to get lonely," is Reed's answer. Nick chimes in, "I'm the one who's lonely, all by myself on the green," and Sarah throws a golf towel at him.

Jenny walks into the bunker holding her sand iron. She carefully digs her feet into the sand to avoid losing her balance while she swings. To avoid the penalty, Jenny doesn't let the clubhead touch the sand before she swings. Jenny's swing slides the clubhead underneath the ball. The force of her swing produces a shower of sand, and the ball comes flying out. Her ball lands on the green and rolls to within 3 feet of the cup. She heaves a big sigh of relief as Reed yells, "Great shot! Hope I can do that."

Reed walks out onto the sand and wiggles his feet into a comfortable stance. "Keep your fingers crossed," he says to his friends. His shot also comes blasting out of the bunker in a spray of sand, but his ball rolls past

MINDING YOUR BUSINESS IN A BUNKER

After a sand shot, it is common courtesy to grab a rake, which should be alongside the bunker, and smooth out the sand.

the cup and about 20 feet down a slope. "At least you're out of there," Sarah says as Reed rakes the sand.

While Jenny and Reed were blasting out of the bunker, Sarah was studying her shot. She wants a chip shot that will land and roll to the cup. She swings her 9-iron and gently launches the ball. It lands about 20 feet from the cup. The ball rolls down a small slope to within 10 feet of the cup.

Reed will putt first. Since Jenny's ball is the closest to the hole, she pulls the flagstick from the cup and

PATCHING PITCH MARKS

When a golf ball lands on the green, it will leave a small depression. Repair these pitch marks so other golfers will have a smooth surface on which to putt. Stick a tee into the edges of the mark. Gently push the sides into the middle. Then, take your putter and lightly tap the repaired area. Golf tradition says that players repair their own marks.

lays it down on the edge of the green. She's careful to keep it out of the way of any of the putts.

Reed was studying the uphill slope he faces while Sarah was chipping on the green. He stands over the ball and strokes a few practice putts. He aims for the right of the cup and strokes the ball firmly, but not too hard. Reed's ball climbs up the slope and curves to the left, but rolls to a stop 2 feet short of the cup.

Nick was carefully surveying the slope of the green as Reed putted. He was trying to imagine how the ball would roll off the slope and into the cup. As he crouches behind the ball, Nick notices that the green slopes from his left to his right. He decides he must start the ball rolling about 6 inches to the left of the cup.

Nick walks up to the ball and takes two practice strokes, all the while thinking about how hard he should swing the putter. He carefully aims the club and gently swings the putter. The ball rolls on the path he had chosen. Soon he hears the gentle "plop" of the ball falling into the metal cup. A birdie! He has beaten the hole by using one stroke less than par. "Wow, way to go Nick!" "Nice shot buddy!" Nick grins as his friends congratulate him.

"OK, Sarah, sink this one," Nick says as Sarah steps up to her ball. She has a 10-foot putt, but she thinks it's a straight-on shot. She bends over the ball, slowly draws back her putter, and taps the ball. Sarah holds her breath as her ball heads straight for the hole, catches the lip of the cup, and bounces just inches from it. "Tough break!"

Jenny faces a 3-foot putt up the slope. She thinks that the slope is not going to make the ball curve. She pictures the ball rolling into the hole as she practices her stroke. Her stroke is firm and smooth, the ball comes off the putter and rolls right into the center of the cup. She picks her ball out of the hole as Nick congratulates her for saving par.

Then Reed steps up for his second putt. This time the ball is about 2 feet from the cup. He taps the ball, gently but firmly, and sighs with relief as it falls into the cup. "OK Sarah, finish it off," he says as he picks up the flagstick. Sarah taps in her ball from 6 inches away, and Reed replaces the flagstick.

The four friends step away from the green so that the players behind them can hit onto the green. But before going on to the next hole, they pause to record their scores. "You're the bogey man, Reed," Nick says. "Oh yeah, well just watch me on this hole. I love these par 5s," Reed says, smiling. "I'm staying out of trouble on this one," Jenny vows. "No rough and no sand for me!"

If you want to test your abilities—like Reed, Nick, Jenny, and Sarah—pick up a club and head for the golf course or the practice range. With blue sky above you and green grass beneath your feet, you'll discover how challenging and fun playing golf can be.

GOLF TALK

backswing: The motion of the golfer and club that brings the club away from the ball and up.

birdie: A score one stroke under par.

bogey: A score that is one stroke more than par.

bunker: A depression filled with sand in a fairway or next to a green.

chip: A short, low shot that is made from close to the green, intended to roll across the green after it lands.

course: A series of holes, usually 18 but sometimes 9, that are laid out over a grassy area. The holes are numbered consecutively.

cup: The 4¼-inch hole on a green into which the ball is hit.

divot: A piece of turf that is dug up by a clubhead during a swing.

downswing: The motion of the golfer and club that brings the club down and toward the ball.

drive: The first shot hit by a golfer on each hole.

eagle: A score that is two shots less than par.

face: The surface of the clubhead that strikes the ball.

fairway: The area between the tee box and the green. The grass on the fairway is cut shorter than the rough but not as short as the green.

follow-through: The motion of the golfer and club that completes a swing after the ball has been hit.

green: A smooth area around the cup where the grass is cut very short.

grip: The way a golfer holds a club. Also, the portion of a club a golfer holds.

handicap: The average number of strokes over par a golfer plays that is subtracted from that player's score when competing.

hazard: An obstacle to make playing more difficult, such as a bunker or a pond.

heel: The portion of the club that joins the shaft to the clubhead.

hole: An area of a course, defined at the start by the tee box and at the finish by the green, over which a golfer hits the ball. Also, the cup on a green.

hole in one: A first stroke on a hole that knocks the ball in the cup.

hook: A shot that curves from right to left in the air.

iron: A club with a thin metal head and a grooved face that is tilted.

links: Originally a course on sandy strips of land between the ocean and the mainland. Links is a nickname for any course.

loft: The angle between a club's shaft and clubhead. The greater the angle, the higher the ball will fly.

out of bounds: An area where play is not allowed.

par: The number of strokes a golfer is expected to use to complete a hole. Par is set for each hole, depending on its length.

penalty stroke: A stroke added to a player's score who broke a rule.

pin: A 6-foot pole with a flag at the top that is stuck in each cup to mark the cup's location.

pitch: A short, high shot, usually hit over a hazard intended not to roll when it lands on the green.

point of impact: The part of the golf swing when the club face and the ball connect.

putt: A stroke used on the green to roll the ball toward the cup.

putter: A club with a long, flat hitting surface to roll the ball on the green.

rough: The area where grass and weeds aren't mowed that often has bushes and trees.

round: A complete game (18 holes).

set-up: The position a golfer assumes before hitting the ball.

slice: A shot that curves from left to right.

stroke: The motion used to hit the ball. Also called a swing.

takeaway: The early part of the backswing during which the club is pulled back away from the ball.

tee: A small wooden or plastic peg on which the ball is placed before the first shot of a hole.

tee box: The marked area at the start of a hole from which a golfer's first shot is hit.

toe: The part of the clubhead farthest from the shaft.

wood: A club with a large clubhead and a flat hitting surface.

FURTHER READING

Anderson, Dave. *The Story of Golf.* New York: William Morrow, 1998.

Ballesteros, Seve. *Trouble-Shooting.* New York: Broadway Books, 1996.

Gordon, John. *The Kids Book of Golf.* Toronto: Kids Can Press, 2001.

Hull, Mary. *The Composite Guide to Golf.* Philadelphia: Chelsea House, 1998.

Uschan, Michael. *Golf.* San Diego: Lucent Books, 2001.

FOR MORE INFORMATION

American Junior Golf Association
1980 Sports Club Drive
Braselton, GA 30517
www.ajga.org

Ladies Professional Golf Association
100 International Golf Drive
Daytona Beach, FL 32124
www.lpga.com

Professional Golfers' Association
100 Avenue of the Champions
Palm Beach Gardens, FL 33418
www.pga.com

United States Golf Association
1 Liberty Corner Road
Far Hills, NJ 07931
www.usga.org

INDEX

backswing, 23, 25
balls, 13, 14
birdie, 34
bogey, 34
bunker, 42, 48–49, 56

chip, 39–40, 56–57
clubhead, 14–16, 23, 46
clubs, 13–17
course, 8, 31–33
cup, 33

divot, 54
downswing, 23, 26, 43
drive, 32

eagle, 34, 52
etiquette, 35–37

face, 16, 21, 23, 27
fairway, 32–33, 55
flange, 16
follow-through, 23, 28, 40, 43

green, 32–33, 37, 44–45, 58
grip, 14, 20–21, 40, 42

handicap, 34
handle, 14
hazard, 32–33, 42
heel, 16–17
hole, 31
hole in one, 52
hook, 17

iron, 14–16, 29, 42, 49, 55

Ladies Professional Golf Association, 10–11
links, 8
loft, 16
Lopez, Nancy, 11, 13

MacDonald, Charles, 8
match play, 33

Morris, Tom, Sr., 8
Nicklaus, Jack, 10
out of bounds, 33

paganica, 8
par, 34
penalty stroke, 35–36, 48
pin, 33
pitch, 42–43, 58
pitching wedge, 16
point of impact, 23, 27
practice range, 20
Professional Golfers' Association of America, 10
putt, 34, 37, 39, 44–47, 57–60
putter, 14–16

Reid, John, 8, 9
rough, 32–33, 53, 56
round, 31
rules, 35–37

sand wedge, 16, 49
Scotland, 8, 10, 31
set-up, 20, 22, 26
shaft, 14, 23
shoes, 13
slice, 17, 53
stroke, 31
stroke play, 33

takeaway, 23–24, 26, 28
tee, 32, 58
tee box, 32, 51–52
toe, 16–17

United States Golf Association, 8–9

Wanamaker, Rodman, 10
wood, 14–16
Woods, Tiger, 19